RISE AND SHINE

HELEN JULIET

LUCA

OF ALL THE WAYS LUCA EXPECTED TO BE WOKEN UP, GETTING his nose licked wasn't one of them.

His eyes flew open, but then he immediately screwed them up against the harsh sunlight streaming through the pulled blinds. His teeth were furry, and his throat felt like crushed glass, but that paled in comparison to the throbbing headache that was making him feel like his skull was trying to force its way free of his head.

What the hell had happened last night?

Luca rubbed his eyes and tried blinking them open again. It was at this moment he realised two things.

One, he was staring into a pair of big brown eyes.

Two, he had absolutely no idea where he was.

Zero.

Unfortunately, the owner of the brown eyes wasn't going to be much help, as they also had a big wet nose and a wagging tail that was currently thumping on the ground, not improving Luca's headache situation at all. The chocolate Labrador panted and gave a little yelp, like they were saying hello.

Luca closed his eyes and wondered if he might actually be dreaming.

But there was no escaping that headache. This was real. He was really in a strange bed, in a strange room, with a dog he'd never seen before in his life.

He was really screwed.

Panic tried to claw its way up Luca's throat, but he managed to keep it at bay, just for now. There *had* to be a logical explanation for this, didn't there? He needed to start with what he did know other than he'd never seen this room or its dog before in his life.

He rubbed his chin, feeling the scruff there. The bed he was in was clean, at least, the sheets cool against his nearly naked body. All he was wearing was his boxers, which was mildly disconcerting. Where were his clothes?

Sitting up and looking around, he couldn't see any of them. But he did make a couple of assumptions about his current location.

The bedroom had bookcases and a treadmill, which suggested to Luca that he was in a house or flat rather than a hotel or anything. The heavy traffic and regular enough sirens through the closed window told him he was almost certainly still in London.

But *where?*

He rubbed his chest, feeling tight as the fear bubbled up again. How did he get here? What was going *on?*

Closing his eyes, he recalled what he could from the night before. It was all so hazy, which wasn't an experience he was used to. He'd never been a heavy drinker and wasn't sure why he would have had anything more than a couple of beers, like usual.

Bloody hell. It had been his *birthday*, hadn't it? How could he have forgotten that, for crying out loud?

A cold, wet nose against the back of his hand startled him.

He gasped, opening his eyes and jerking his arm back, the sudden movement making his head pound harder. The dog whimpered and butted their head against Luca's thigh under the duvet.

Luca sighed, a smile twitching at his lips despite his pain and confusion. He petted the dog's head. The situation couldn't be *that* bad if this was his welcome committee, could it?

He realised the dog was wearing a collar, so he turned it until he found the name tag.

"Briar," he said out loud. The dog immediately perked their ears up. Somehow, knowing their name made Luca slightly less afraid. "Hey there, Briar. Where's your mum or dad, hmm?"

Briar's long, heavy tail wagged happily at Luca's words, and they barked a couple of times.

A sudden realisation smacked Luca so hard he clutched his chest again. If his clothes weren't here, then where was his phone? Not to mention his wallet and keys. Panic overwhelmed his already nauseous body, and for a second he thought he might throw up. But a frantic glance to the bedside cabinet soothed him.

Not only was his phone lying there, perfectly fine, but it was plugged into a charger. His wallet was next to his keys and the chewing gum he'd forgotten he'd slipped into his pocket. Likewise, he also saw the condom he remembered grabbing at the last minute in case he managed to get lucky. It had been his birthday, after all. The shiny wrapper glinted in the morning sunshine, and for some reason, Luca blushed. He didn't have anything to be ashamed of, but still, the thought of a stranger seeing that was somehow a little too intimate.

His phone was blinking, and as soon as Luca unlocked it, he was bombarded with messages on several different platforms. Text, WhatsApp, Facebook, Instagram – all his inboxes had several, if not dozens of notifications, all from people asking the same questions:

Luca, where are you?

Are you okay babe?

We can't find you!

Luca! Pick up your phone!

I'm worried hun, my calls are going straight to voicemail. Is your phone dead?

WHERE! ARE! YOU?

Luca felt sick. Everyone had been so worried. All his friends who had come out to celebrate had been running around trying to find him in the small hours of the morning, and he couldn't even remember where he'd been or what he'd been doing.

Or who he'd been with.

The most worried had been his three cousins: Florence, Fiona, and Maryanne. They were all older than him and had fussed over him since he'd been born, nicknaming themselves his fairy godmothers. Between them, they had sent him almost a hundred messages.

It appeared they hadn't slept. Fiona, the oldest and bossiest of them, was threatening to punch him if he didn't answer soon, whilst the others were ringing around local hospitals. Mortified, he messaged their group chat back first.

I'm okay. I'm SO sorry to have scared you. But I'm fine, I promise. I'll explain as soon as I can.

When he had an explanation to give.

He knew that wouldn't satisfy his cousins, but they weren't the only ones who'd been fretting over his fate. He pinged the same few words to other chats to reach as many people as possible, hoping reading their messages might jolt his memory and fill in some of the blanks. But it was like he'd just *lost* twelve hours, and in its place was a throbbing headache that was getting worse by the minute.

As soon as he stopped guiltily obsessing over his phone, though, he realised there were other things on the bedside cabinet.

Very useful things.

A glass of water had been left on a coaster. There was also a packet of ibuprofen...and a folded-up note.

'Good morning!' it said on the front in unfamiliar handwriting.

Luca blinked, surprised he hadn't noticed that sooner. But he was feeling rough as balls, so he grabbed the painkillers and knocked two back before chugging half the pint of water in one go. He gasped gratefully and wiped his mouth with the back of his hand, then carefully picked up the note.

If someone had bothered to write him a note, maybe he'd get some answers. Hopefully he had been saved by one of his friends whose home he'd never been to before.

A sudden thought frightened the shit out of him.

Nothing had...*happened* when he'd blacked out, had it? If this was a friend's place or not, it didn't matter. He felt sick at the thought that someone might have taken advantage of him whilst he'd been unconscious or too out of it. But a quick squirm of his bum against the mattress told him he hadn't had sex, at least not penetrative. He breathed a small sigh of relief, taking a few breaths to try and calm his heart rate. There was still no guarantee that something unwanted hadn't taken place whilst he'd been blacked out, but at least he appeared to have dodged one of the worse things that might have happened.

He felt a flare of anger at himself, but almost immediately he quashed it. He *knew* he hadn't gotten off-his-face drunk, so there had to be another explanation.

Speaking of which, he finally opened the note. A part of

him was scared of what it was going to say, but his desperation to discover anything he could outweighed his fear.

"Here we go," he said to Briar, who thumped their tail.

'Hi, there!' Well, that was a cheerful enough start. Whoever this was, hopefully they weren't pissed off at Luca.

'You're probably wondering where you are. Don't worry. Everything's okay! My name's Ryan and this is my flat. I was the bouncer at the club you were at last night. You were in a bad way. Your phone was dead, you couldn't tell me your address to get a taxi, and there didn't seem to be anyone at the club who knew you. So I said I'd look after you, and you agreed. Hopefully you don't mind.'

Whoever Ryan was had drawn a smiley face there, but Luca's heart still skipped a beat as shame crept over him. How could he have lost control that badly? If all his friends and cousins had been looking for him, why hadn't the bouncer seen them? It didn't make any sense. He sipped some more water and continued reading.

'I thought I'd give you some space, so I've gone to the gym. Feel free to slip out (Elephant and Castle tube is a five-minute walk away) or stay and have some breakfast or even go back to sleep. If you venture out of the room, though, just beware of my dog. He's very friendly, but I know not everyone likes dogs, so I've shut your bedroom door.'

Luca raised an eyebrow at Briar, who looked back with a perfectly innocent expression. "That door was shut, huh, mate?" Briar barked and chased his tail once in a circle. Luca managed a weak chuckle, not actually cross. "You're a clever boy. Yes, you are," he cooed, giving the lab another stroke before reading the rest of the note.

'You were a bit sick on your clothes, so I hope you don't mind, but I put them in the washer-dryer. They should be done by mid-morning. If I don't see you, take care and get home safe!

Rx'

"Fuck," Luca rasped out loud, consumed by humiliation as he rubbed his head, still waiting for the painkillers to kick in. So…he *had* been totally shit-faced. Maybe his friends had bought him shots or something? But surely if they had, he'd remember the before, if not the after?

Whoever Ryan was, he must see his fair share of drunk people at work. Did he have a habit of taking the really battered ones home with him? Or had Luca been *that* bad. He groaned and rubbed his sore eyes. At least he hadn't ended up in hospital, getting his stomach pumped. But this wasn't much better.

He sighed and finished his water, already feeling slightly less like death warmed up. He was still very uncomfortable that he'd somehow got into such a state, but at least he'd been lucky enough to encounter what read like a true good Samaritan. Part of him considered sticking around to thank the guy in person, but his embarrassment got the better of him.

"Oh!" he said out loud and smiled at Briar. "I could write a note back," he said happily. He'd hate this guy to feel like Luca was ungrateful, but he didn't think he could stand looking Ryan in the eyes if Luca had been so drunk that he'd thrown up.

He still wasn't sure how that could have happened, but he had time to mull over that later. First things first, he needed to venture out and find wherever the washer-dryer was and hope that his clothes were recovered. He might even be cheeky and see if there was some toothpaste in the bathroom that he could run over his teeth with his finger to at least attempt to get rid of some of the fuzz.

In just his underwear, he slipped out of the bed and

padded over the soft carpet to the door that Briar had left ajar. The lab followed obediently by his side, looking up at Luca with his tongue lolling out of the side of his mouth.

Luca peeked out.

The flat was quiet.

He let out a sigh of relief. It looked like Ryan was still at the gym, giving Luca the privacy he needed to explore the apartment.

It wasn't large. He guessed he'd been in the spare bedroom, and now he was looking at a short corridor with three other doors. He made an educated guess that these were the main bedroom, bathroom, and kitchen-cum-living room.

Taking a deep breath, Luca tiptoed into the hall, still nervous despite being pretty certain that he and Briar were alone. Glancing at the walls, he saw a few framed photos of landscapes, as well as a group shot of a dozen people in snow gear, waving to the camera from the top of a mountain. Luca peered at it briefly, wondering if one of them was Ryan. But there would be no way to know, even if all their faces weren't obscured by skiing goggles. Maybe there would be other photos of Luca's mysterious saviour around the flat…

No. He wasn't here to snoop. That would be awful. This guy had already done so much for Luca. The least Luca could do would be to make himself scarce before any awkward reunion took place. The washer-dryer would probably be in the kitchen, so that's where he headed.

Still, it was kind of nice to know *something* about Ryan. He was obviously into the outdoors and looked like the adventurous type. Luca also spied some sort of sporting medals hanging up from a display as he walked quietly into the kitchen.

Then he stopped at the fucking *sword* hanging on the wall.

Blinking, several times, he then looked down at Briar, as

if he might provide some answers. Unsurprisingly, the dog just kept gently wagging his big tail, smiling up at Luca. Luca bit his lip and turned his gaze back to the wall. Who had an honest-to-god sword in their flat? Should Luca be trying to flee out of Ryan's front door faster? Was this guy a nut job? Luca peered closer at the thing and, on a wild whim, touched the side of the blade.

It was blunt.

He stared at his fingers, mildly horrified at himself. What if it *had* been sharp. Fucking hell, he really was hungover. But his closer inspection had at least assuaged his fears a little that he'd accidentally been taken home by a serial killer or some kind of vigilante. The thing had a leather handle and strange symbols down the centre of the blade. It was most likely a prop from a film or TV show.

Sure enough, when Luca ventured into the kitchen and living room area, the first thing he saw was a Gollum figure crouched on one of the shelves, then a framed Fellowship of the Ring poster above a long, waist-high cabinet filled with DVDs.

"Aww," Luca said to Briar with a little chuckle. "Your daddy's a nerd."

For some reason, that warmed Luca's heart. He'd promised not to snoop and told himself it didn't matter who Ryan was beyond his white knight in shining armour. But he kind of already liked this bouncer who climbed mountains and collected geeky memorabilia.

The kitchen and living room space was divided by a sofa with a dining room table positioned longways off the back of one couch. A large TV sat next to balcony doors, looking out on the third or fourth floor on an undistinguishable view of London. A second sofa was positioned by the first in an L-shape so they both faced the telly. A few plants looked green and fresh in pots on the carpet and the shelves, clearly well looked after, and there was a bird feeder hanging out on the balcony.

"Huh," said Luca with a little smile. It was kind of sad he wasn't going to get to meet Ryan. He seemed like a fun, interesting, caring sort of guy.

For a fleeting second, Luca wondered what someone would think if they woke up in his tiny room in a town house in Hackney that he shared with four other people. It was overflowing with fabrics, resource books, and folder upon folder of designs and patterns, but not much else. He had to be creative with what space he had around the single bed for how he stored all his clothes, shoes, toiletries, and laptop.

There wasn't much room for sentimentality when you lived in a shoebox.

He sighed and imagined for a second what it might be like to afford a two-bedroom apartment in London all by yourself. *Well, not quite,* Luca thought as he bent down and scratched between Briar's ears. One income, at least.

All right, he needed to stop wandering around a stranger's home in his underwear and find his clothes so he could get out of here. It was stupid, but the thought of going back to the shoebox didn't really inspire much joy. Perhaps he could go see one of his friends or cousins on the way back to his place? After the fright he'd given them all, that was probably a very good idea.

He could tell his phone was blowing up with messages again, even though it was on silent. The screen kept flashing where Luca was clutching it in his hand, but for now, he ignored them (especially the one he glimpsed from Fiona, threatening to wring his neck for scaring them all so much).

They would all have to wait until Luca had some clothes on. He was starting to shiver, even though the flat wasn't particularly cold. It was probably because he was tired and dehydrated. He located the washing machine easy enough, and it wasn't spinning, so he yanked at the door.

It refused to budge.

Luca groaned. Studying the console, he was pretty sure that the cycle was almost done, but the machine was just finishing off Luca's clothes. The only option available to him was to wait.

Well, he could at least wrap a blanket around himself. He was pretty sure there had been one over the bed he'd woken up in, so he headed back into the hallway, glancing at the only closed door, next to the bathroom.

That must have been Ryan's room.

Luca paused. The temptation to take a quick peek was big, but Briar whined at his feet and reminded Luca of just how unethical that would be. Just because he was desperate to put a face to the name, note, and flat didn't give him any right to poke around. He shook his head at himself for even considering it.

Instead, he walked back towards the spare room.

Just as the front door swung open right in front of him.

2

LUCA

There was no time to think. Dashing to either the bathroom or the bedroom would have taken several steps either way, and if he'd gone back into the kitchen, there would have been nowhere to hide. Luca's hungover brain was too tired to consider anything else other than to gasp and throw his hands over his crotch as his and Ryan's eyes locked in surprise.

In the awful, horrible pause that followed, a single thought flooded Luca's mind.

Ryan was *drop-dead gorgeous.*

He wasn't a regular bouncer at the bars Luca usually went to, he was sure. He knew a lot of them by sight, and he would *definitely* have remembered this guy. He was too big to forget.

Luca put Ryan at just over six foot, with broad shoulders and muscular arms clearly visible under his light grey hoodie. His skin was dark, and his wide eyes a warm, hazel brown. His hair was short at the back and sides, but the dreadlocks on top of his head were pulled in with a band and fell just above his ears.

For a second that seemed to stretch for eternity, they just

stared at each other. Then Briar gave a loud bark, making both men jump as the dog dashed over to his daddy. "Hey, boy," Ryan said breathlessly. He dropped his duffle bag to the floor to pet his dog, then glanced back up at Luca. "Glad to see you're awake and okay."

"Uhh…" Luca croaked, wondering if it was possible to die from embarrassment. Then his feet finally caught up with his brain, and he bolted into the spare bedroom and slammed the door behind him. "Holy fuck, I'm *so* sorry!" he cried through the wood. He was so mortified tears were springing in his eyes. Despite having a solid wall between him and the other man, he was still hugging his slender frame, trying to hide and feeling hot shame as the blush spread over his face, neck, shoulders, and chest. A wave of nausea swept through him, and the pint of water he'd drank with the painkillers threatened to make a reappearance.

There was a tentative knock on the door, accompanied by a whine at the crack by the carpet. "Are you all right?" Ryan asked.

So much for Luca's plan of being dignified and stealthy. He was so ashamed of himself that his throat thickened and his eyes filled again. "I was trying to leave before you came back," he said by way of an answer. "I'm sorry."

There was a pause. "Well, your clothes are still in the machine…" Ryan said slowly.

Luca laughed miserably. "Yeah, I saw."

Another pause. "There's a blanket in the cupboard at the top of the wardrobe," Ryan said gently. He had a soothing, rumbly voice with an accent Luca would place closer to East London than South. Luca breathed deeply, trying to calm himself. Ryan wasn't mad, he was almost certain. "Of course," Ryan continued through the door, "you're totally free to leave as soon as your stuff is dry. But I thought you might want to chat about last night."

Luca bit his lip and blinked back tears. Last night, when he'd humiliated himself. But maybe Ryan had answers that might give Luca some relief from the torment he was putting himself through? He inhaled again, steeling himself, and nodded, even though Ryan couldn't see him.

"One second," Luca called through the wood.

He moved into the room, going to find the blanket Ryan had mentioned. Apparently, Luca had been in such a state that he'd imagined there'd been one on top of the duvet. But sure enough, there was a large fluffy one at the top of the wardrobe that he was just able to pull down and envelope himself with. Sheepishly, he padded back to the door and eased it open, blinking at the face with the raised eyebrows on the other side.

"Hi," said Ryan with a lopsided grin.

With his phone still gripped in his hand, Luca clutched the blanket around him, ensuring he was totally covered. Not that it mattered after Ryan had seen it all just now – not to mention the utter humiliation of realising this stunning man had undressed him before. But it made Luca feel a little less foolish as they stood there awkwardly.

"Hello," Luca rasped, his voice still not quite right. "Sorry about that. I mean…sorry for everything, really." He grimaced.

"You said sorry already. Several times." Ryan chuckled, which made Luca think he was only teasing. "I promise, it's fine. You've got nothing to apologise for." Luca was going to hotly dispute that when Briar pushed the door open further with his big nose and headbutted Luca's thigh. Ryan beamed. "He likes you," he declared.

For some reason, that made Luca proud. But that was stupid. Briar seemed like a very friendly dog. Luca shouldn't be honoured just because Ryan's dog liked him, or think it was *almost* the same as Ryan liking Luca himself.

"He's been taking care of me," Luca said affectionately as he scratched between the dog's ears.

Ryan chuckled. He laughed easily, Luca noticed. "He was supposed to leave you alone. Weren't you, Mr Nosey Pants?" He looked suddenly back up at Luca. "You're not allergic, are you?"

Luca felt a physical pang in his chest. Ryan was so *damned* caring and considerate, but Luca didn't deserve any of that. He'd made a total fool of himself to the extent that Ryan had been forced to put himself out just to make sure Luca hadn't wound up dead in a ditch somewhere.

"No, I'm not allergic," Luca said softly. He bit his lip and cast around for what words he could possibly use to start making his apologies. But then a *ping* noise came from the kitchen, and he felt a thrill of relief rush through him. "Oh! Um. I think my clothes are done?"

Ryan laughed sheepishly and rubbed the back of his neck. "Sort of. They'll need to air a little while before they'll be wearable. The tumble dryer only does so much before it'll start shrinking them. Sorry. I thought you'd sleep in longer. I wish I had something more in your size to offer you."

Luca experienced a moment of panic at having to hang around even longer, but maybe the clothes would be drier than Ryan thought. Or perhaps Luca could stand to put them on a little damp? He had no dignity left by this point, after all.

"You've done more than enough already," he mumbled, trying not to blush again. "Honestly, I feel so embarrassed. I don't know what happened last night."

Ryan huffed and gave Luca that lopsided smile again. "Come on. Let me make you a brew. I'll chuck your clothes onto the drying rack, and we can try and fill in the blanks." Before Luca could protest that he didn't need any *more* kindness from Ryan – he was so indebted already – Briar barked and thumped his tail into the wall as it wagged. Ryan winked. "Briar says that's a brilliant plan."

Luca watched helplessly as Ryan turned and made his way down the hallway, whispering nonsense at his dog, making Briar grin and wag his tail even more as he followed. Biting his lip, Luca realised he didn't have much of a choice other than to follow, so he wrapped the blanket tighter around his shoulders as it billowed around his ankles, and walked after them.

"I, um, don't normally drink a lot," Luca began without being prompted.

He leaned against the kitchen doorframe. Ryan looked over his shoulder at him as he crouched and clicked open the washer-dryer. Luca shifted uncomfortably, not wanting to make excuses, but he felt he had to defend his completely out-of-character actions.

"The last thing I remember was celebrating my birthday-"

"Oh, it's your birthday?" Ryan asked, beaming as he stood back up, clutching Luca's damp and crumpled-up clothes. A sock flopped out over his forearm like a lolling tongue. "Happy birthday, mate."

"Luca," he quickly supplied. "Uh, that's my name. In case I didn't mention it, um, before." *When I was paralytic.*

Ryan tilted his head and nodded. "Happy birthday, *Luca.*" He winked, then busied himself for a few minutes as he yanked out a clothes horse from between the fridge-freezer and the counter, then hung up Luca's things. Good thing, as Luca needed a moment to recover from how hearing Ryan say his name made him feel. He shifted on his feet and hoped his twitching cock wasn't obvious in his underwear. He double-checked the blanket was covering him.

"Anyway, I was at the Rose and Crown, and I guess I lost my friends because-"

Ryan held up his hand, having draped the last of Luca's

clothes over the rack. He gave Luca such a quizzical look, and Luca's words faded in his mouth. "Dreamland."

Luca blinked. "I'm sorry?"

"You were at Dreamland. It's a bar around the corner from the Crown. Is that where you started?"

That water threatened to make an appearance again as horror washed over Luca. How had he ended up in a totally different *bar?* He didn't remember leaving the pub! Holy fuck, this just kept getting worse and worse. He suddenly realised *that* was probably why his friends and three cousins hadn't been able to find him.

"Yeah," he rasped. "Is Dreamland, um, where you found me?"

Ryan sighed and folded his impressive arms. "Yeah, I work at Dreamland. Listen, I don't want to alarm you, but does the name Malcom mean anything to you? There was a guy there who seemed to be upsetting you who bolted when I came over. I think he might have spiked your drink."

All the blood rushed from Luca's head, and he sagged against the doorframe. The nausea was replaced by an icy coldness that made him shiver.

"Malcom? You're sure?" Ryan nodded. Luca swallowed. "Okay. I think I will have that cup of tea, if that's alright with you?"

Ryan licked his lips. "Sugar?"

Luca laughed hollowly. "Yes. *Lots.*"

3

LUCA

Malcom. Fucking *Malcom*. Luca managed to stumble to the dining room table and sit down, still cocooned in the blanket. He stared at the knots in the wood.

Out of the corner of his eye, he saw Ryan fill the kettle, then flick it on. He gathered up two mugs, tea bags to drop in them, milk, and the bag of sugar. Then, whilst the kettle was only just starting to grumble and hiss, Ryan lowered himself into the seat opposite Luca.

"So," he said, lacing his fingers together and raising an eyebrow. "You know this guy, Malcom?"

Luca laughed ruefully. "You could say that. He's my ex-boyfriend. Turned into a bit of a control freak, so I left."

He didn't worry about outing himself to a near stranger, as Ryan had to already know he was queer from the two gay bars he'd just mentioned being in. But Luca decided not to add that it had taken him several months to muster up the courage to end it for good with his ex. Malcom hadn't wanted to let go. Apparently, he still didn't.

"We broke up about six weeks ago." Luca groaned as a sudden flash of memory came back to him. A flare of anger from the previous night that managed to pierce its way through the hazy fog. "Oh my god, you're right. Malcom was there!" He met eyes with Ryan, nodding. "He was furious he hadn't been invited to my birthday. But I think I was even angrier that he gate-crashed. Then…" *Fuck.* It was all such a blur, but fresh horror was now outweighing his confusion. "He was being nice. Fake nice. He mentioned going to Dreamland, but I don't remember leaving the Crown. You don't really think he put something in my drink, do you?"

Ryan shrugged apologetically as the kettle pinged to announce it was boiled. Luca watched Ryan rise to go make up their cups of tea. "I've been doing door work for several years now," Ryan said. "I feel like I can tell if someone's drunk or it's something else. Did you do any drugs last night?" He glanced over his shoulder with a sympathetic look. "No judgements."

"None needed," said Luca with a laugh. "I'm far too boring to pop any pills. I just like a couple of beers." He tutted. "Mal always complained I was a stick-in-the-mud. But…" He bit his lip and shook his head, wrapping his hands around the hot mug Ryan placed in front of him. "To spike my drink? That's crossing a line, even for him."

Ryan sat back in the seat opposite with his own steaming cup and placed the sugar between them. Luca helped himself to three spoonfuls. Then, in a move that seemed to almost stop Luca's heart, Ryan reached out and squeezed Luca's wrist with an affectionate smile. "It's not boring to know what you enjoy and refuse to be put under peer pressure. Good for you." He released Luca's hand and picked up his mug. If he noticed Luca was a little breathless and trembling after their touch, he didn't show it.

Luca cleared his throat. "Well, I feel slightly less humiliated if you really think it wasn't my fault. If you think he…he did this to me."

Ryan nodded. "It's just a guess, but an educated one." He raised his eyebrows. "That's why I was so determined to look after you. I hope you don't think I'm a total nutter who kidnaps nice lads at the weekend for jollies."

"No, no," said Luca urgently. Aside from a fleeting second when he'd seen the sword, Luca definitely didn't think Ryan was dodgy. "Of course not."

He only half registered that Ryan just implied that he was 'nice'. Also, that seemed to answer Luca's earlier question: Ryan did not frequently bring drunk and vulnerable strangers home.

Luca was special.

"You were my knight in shining armour. *Thank* you." He shuddered, his stomach turning over. What the hell had Mal been hoping to achieve by putting anything in Luca's beer? Had he thought they might get back together if Luca was drunk?

Or had Malcom been hoping to take advantage of Luca, just like he'd feared when he'd woken up earlier?

The sob escaped Luca's throat before he even realised his eyes were damp. "Sorry," he whispered, hastily rubbing at them and then covering his face. "I think I'm a bit shocked. That's just horrible." The pressure on his lap made him look down, only to see Briar's big, dark eyes looking sorrowfully back at him from where his head was resting on Luca's leg. He whimpered, his big tail drooping down for once. "Oh, it's okay, boy," Luca whispered, gently stroking his head.

When Ryan reached out this time, Luca wasn't so jumpy. In fact, he welcomed the warm skin-on-skin contact. He raised his sore eyes and sniffed, offering Ryan a little smile, which Ryan returned tenfold. "I knew that Malcom was a limp-dicked tool," he said wisely.

Luca burst out laughing, which felt like a strange relief after the stress of the morning so far. "He completely was," he agreed. "And terrible in bed." Oh *fuck!* Why was he talking about sex in front of Ryan? "Uh, I mean, that's why I dumped him. Well, that and the being crazy controlling and fucking weird part. I always suspected, but now…" He trailed off, his throat threatening to clamp up again.

Before he could get melancholy, though, Ryan squeezed his arm. "You're well shot of him, mate," he said kindly. Then he bit his lip and narrowed his eyes for just a second. "Look, this is stupid. You probably have plans. But I was going to have a lazy day. If you wanted to hang around while your clothes dried and you recuperated, I was thinking maybe of ordering far too much pizza and playing video games. It would be nice to have some company."

He raised his eyebrows. Meanwhile, Luca's heart flipped over. Ryan wanted to *what?* What had he just invited Luca to do? *Stay?*

"Huh?" Luca uttered stupidly.

Ryan laughed and withdrew his hand, immediately making Luca's insides clench miserably. "No worries. It was silly. You probably feel rough and have to get home."

Luca just gaped for a moment. "I mean, yeah," he agreed. "I feel proper rough. But I think I might commit murder for pizza right now. Oh! And those little cheesy jalapeño things in breadcrumbs. In fact, anything dripping with cheese. Holy *fuck.*" He rubbed his temples and moaned, his stomach growling.

Then he realised what he'd said.

Dripping with cheese? He might as well have begged Ryan to come all over him. Mortified, he felt his cheeks heating up. "Uh, I mean…"

Ryan laughed – properly, not just a chuckle. He grinned at Luca. "A man after my own heart, I see."

Speaking of hearts, Luca's very unhelpfully flipped again. Shit. He liked Ryan laughing way too much, considering how kind and selfless he'd been towards Luca. The last thing he'd surely want was the guy he'd unwillingly brought home to start fawning over him.

Except…he was directly asking Luca to stay, wasn't he?

"I feel like I've been an awful burden and caused you so much trouble already," Luca blurted out. Then he thrust out the phone that was still in his hand and met Ryan's gaze. "Let *me* order the pizza, please. It's the very least I can do to express my immense gratitude."

A smile spread slowly over Ryan's face. "So you'll stay?" He gestured to the chocolate Labrador snuggled up by Luca's feet. "I mean, Briar would be thrilled if you did."

Luca chuckled and reached down to pet the big dog's head. "Well, if it would make *Briar* happy, then, yes. Of course."

He and Ryan held each other's gazes for just a little longer than Luca would have expected. Then Luca blinked and cleared his throat, smiling sheepishly at him.

"So, what do you want? On your *pizza*," he spluttered for clarification.

Ryan's smile was different this time. It was slower and… something else. "Everything," he said simply.

Everything, huh?

Luca could work with that.

4

RYAN

Was Ryan being a complete idiot? Or worse, a creep? He hoped not.

Because as he watched Luca concentrating on their pizza order on his phone, absently stroking Ryan's beloved Briar's head, something funny was happening with Ryan's heart.

And his cock.

It was like a stirring, all the way through him. He'd felt sympathy the night before when poor Luca had been so out of it and clearly distressed. But this was more than obligation or responsibility that Ryan was feeling now. As his eyes grazed over Luca's slender frame and his tousled auburn hair, Ryan's heart ached in a different way that went beyond mere protection.

It was longing.

But that was wrong. Luca had been through a nasty ordeal and a terrible fright. He must have been pretty freaked out this morning when he woke up in Ryan's flat. But slowly, he was starting to relax. Even if it was just by millimetres, Ryan could see his shoulders lowering under the blanket. That didn't mean he was interested in Ryan in any way, though, and that *certainly* wasn't why Ryan had taken it upon himself to bring the other man back home with him. That had just been the right thing to do.

There was just...*something* about Luca that was making Ryan's heart beat a little faster. It was difficult not to feel kindly towards anyone who was nice to his dog. But it wasn't just that. Ryan liked the way Luca's green eyes lit up when he stopped worrying and apologising. Ryan hadn't had a clue what effect suggesting ordering pizza would have on Luca, but it had been dazzling. Ryan liked guys who were enthusiastic about food or anything really. Life was too short not to follow your passions.

He found himself sitting there, nursing his cooling tea, wanting to know so much more about Luca. He was obviously strong enough to escape a controlling and manipulative relationship with that twat, Malcom. A fierce protectiveness uncurled in Ryan's chest. He never wanted *anyone* to harm Luca like that again. Which was kind of ridiculous – Luca wouldn't stay after his clothes were dry. He had a life to get back to.

Except...Luca sighed and smiled as he finally closed his phone, shaking his head. "Sorry. Pizza's all ordered. I just had to reply to some messages as well. My cousins are like my big sisters, and they get scary when they worry too much about me." He laughed and rubbed the back of his head. "Are you sure you're okay with me staying?"

Ryan grinned, his heart fluttering just a little. "Hell yeah," he said enthusiastically. "I'm always bloody working and never think to have people over. It's always easier to meet in central, you know?"

Luca nodded, biting his lip as his eyes shone with interest. *God*, he was cute. "So you're on the door at Dreamland a lot?"

Ryan shook his head. "Only Saturdays and Tuesdays. I

work a few other clubs, freelance, and during the day, I'm a personal trainer. I run a few spin classes, too."

Luca's eyebrows disappeared into his thick, messy hair. Ryan's fingers itched to run his hands through it.

He sat on them until he calmed down.

"Wow, that's awesome," Luca said. "No wonder you're in such great shape. I mean! Uh…" Luca was so adorable when he blushed under the few freckles across his nose and cheeks. "Sorry. Not that I was looking."

Ryan arched an eyebrow at him. "Did you just apologise for saying I've got a great body?" he teased, delighted when Luca's blush deepened. He was grinning back at Ryan, though, and the air felt like it crackled between them with electricity. Was Ryan imaging this? He didn't want to make things up when Luca had just been through an ordeal with his ex. But it did *feel* like there was a kind of pull between them.

"Apologising is kind of my thing," said Luca playfully, rolling his eyes. "Haven't you realised that yet? It works *way* better than flirting."

Flirting? Was that what he was doing? Because if he was, Ryan was interested. *Very* interested.

But he was getting ahead of himself. Ryan laughed, pushing away any thoughts of flirting. Mostly. "Is that so?"

Luca nodded. "You should try it sometime. It'll make the lads swoon."

So much for forgetting about flirting.

For a moment, their gazes lingered together as their smiles faded. Ryan wasn't sure about Luca, but he could feel his gentle ribbing morphing into something a little more heated.

Except, he was looking after Luca here, and he needed to be responsible. The last thing the poor guy wanted after blacking out and getting lost was to be hit on whilst hardly wearing any clothes.

Ryan cleared his throat. "So. How long until the pizza arrives?"

Luca blinked, maybe thrown by the shift in conversation. "Oh, uh, another twenty-five minutes."

"Great." Ryan nodded. "Well, would you like to take a shower? I think I might even have a spare toothbrush lying around. Then I *might* have a pair of my sister's jogging bottoms in a drawer somewhere that you could borrow until your clothes are dry." He wished he'd remembered those earlier. He hated seeing Luca uncomfortable.

At the mention of a shower, Luca groaned, which didn't help the uncomfortable tightness that was increasing in Ryan's jeans. "Holy shit, I'd *love* a shower. Thank you." Ryan expected Luca to protest that Ryan had already done enough again, but he didn't. That warmed Ryan's heart. He wanted Luca to accept his help, to allow Ryan to care for him.

"Let me grab you some things. Then I'll pop out with Briar to give him a run around the grassy area outside." At the mention of his name, Briar lifter his head and barked, wagging his tail. "Yes, yes, all right," Ryan said good-naturedly. "You'd think you were never, *ever* walked."

Luca shook his head with a serious expression. "Briar told me his daddy is very mean and never takes him out. In fact, he said he's kept locked up in this tower!"

Oh, *fuck*. Luca has a silly side to him as well. Ryan's heart gave a little squeeze. He knew he shouldn't be thinking like this, but he couldn't help it.

Luca was gorgeous, in so many ways.

Ryan shifted in his seat. Fresh air. That would sort his muddled head out. And his cock. "Is that so? Well, Daddy better prove Briar wrong, hadn't he?"

Briar barked and ran around in a circle, then dashed off

to pick up his lead like he always did before a walk. Ryan and Luca watched him go fondly. Then Ryan hastily started tidying up their tea mugs so as to avoid another charged, silent look between them.

"Give me a sec, and I'll hunt down that toothbrush," Ryan said as he loaded the dishwasher. "I'm sure it's somewhere. I just need to look. Well, obviously, it's not going to jump out at me all by itself." He was babbling to try and keep the tentative easy atmosphere going. He wanted Luca to feel comfortable.

He wanted Luca to stay.

"That would be amazing," Luca said with a shy laugh. "My teeth feel like caterpillars."

That's no good for kissing, Ryan's brain unhelpfully supplied. There was going to be *no* kissing, he told himself firmly.

Instead, he smiled at Luca's excitement over cleaning his teeth and led the way out to the cupboard where he kept his spare towels, loo roll, and anything else that would otherwise clutter up the bathroom.

"Here you go," he said triumphantly, glad he'd bought a twin set when he'd last picked up a manual toothbrush for his travel wash kit. He handed it to Luca, along with a clean bath towel. "I'll go see if my sister did leave those joggers here for lounging in. If not, I'm sure your clothes will be dry soon, and, um…"

His thoughts trailed off as he became consumed with the realisation that Luca was standing there in just a blanket and his underwear right now. But in mere moments, he was going to be naked and wet, all that creamy skin getting rosy and flushed under the hot water. Ryan wondered if he had more freckles. He'd tried not to look last night when he'd been taking care of Luca's clothes, and this morning he'd moved too fast in the hallway to really see. But Ryan could just imagine a smattering of delicious freckles across his shoulders to match the ones over his nose. What would they be like to touch? To kiss…?

"Ryan?" said Luca uncertainly. *Fuck.* He'd been staring.

"Right, yes, sorry. Let me just…"

Ryan dashed into the spare room. Sure enough, his sister had stashed a couple of things for when she crashed over. Ryan snatched the joggers, T-shirt, and socks up from the drawer, then rushed back out to Luca.

"I'll leave you to it," Ryan said as he thrust the things into Luca's hands, then backed into the wall, making his photo frames rattle. *Bollocks.* "Come on, Briar! Do you want to go for a walk? Here, boy!" He whistled, grateful he still had his keys in his pocket and his shoes on his feet. As Briar came bounding back out of Ryan's bedroom, the lead in his mouth, all Ryan had to grab was doggy treats and baggies from the table by the door. "See you in a minute!" he called out to Luca.

Then he was out in the corridor, his door shut safely behind them.

"Get a *grip*," he muttered out loud to himself. He'd be lucky now if he hadn't scared Luca off.

Praying he'd still be there when he got back, Ryan jogged down the stairs with Briar at his side, hoping he hadn't just spoiled everything between them before it had really had a chance to begin.

5

LUCA

Luca felt a little tingly, and for the first time that morning, it wasn't because of his hangover. Was it his imagination, or had Ryan just been jittery around him? Nervous, even?

Why would that be?

Luca wanted to guess, but the lure of the shower was calling to him. So he locked the door, hung up both the blanket and the towel on the back of the door, placed the clean clothes on the closed toilet seat, and got the water running as hot as he could stand it. As the room started steaming up, Luca looked at himself in the mirror before his reflection disappeared in the fog.

Could Ryan really be interested in him like *that?*

Luca tried to see himself with a stranger's eyes. He was slim, but he wasn't scrawny. He had a little bulk on him. Growing up, he'd been incredibly self-conscious of his freckles– to the extent he'd scrubbed himself bloody one particularly awful day – but now he loved them. They were a unique map of his skin. He touched his chest, tracing his fingers over the smooth, marked skin. What did Ryan think of them? He must have seen them at some point.

Groaning, Luca grabbed the toothpaste and squeezed a dollop onto the new brush Ryan had just given him and cleaned his teeth vigorously. His cock was throbbing and his whole body felt quivery. He knew he was tired and hungover, but he couldn't seem to stop his physical reaction.

To be fair, Ryan was hot. *So* hot. And Luca was only human. Why shouldn't he admit he fancied him a little? Nothing was going to happen between them. It didn't hurt to dream that it *could*, though.

After rinsing his mouth, Luca divested himself of his underwear. Then he hopped under the stream and sighed as the water hit his skin. Immediately feeling less grotty, he lathered shampoo and conditioner through his hair before soaping up his body.

Oh, what the hell. He was alone until Ryan and Briar got back. He wasn't hurting anyone. And after the shit his ex had put him through last night, Luca figured he deserved a bit of self-care.

He took his cock in hand and let his eyes drift close.

In his imagination, Ryan was there behind him, kissing his neck and stroking Luca's hardening dick with his strong hand. Luca ran his hand over his chest, the water cascading over his fingers as he tweaked and pinched his nipples, sending little shocks down to his groin. His balls tingled in anticipation. As he wanked off, he pictured all kinds of scenarios. He'd drop to his knees for Ryan and suck him off. But not too much, because then Ryan would push him against the wall and finger him until Luca was ready to take his cock.

Luca bit his lip as he fingered himself instead, jerking his hand faster as he stroked his prostate. His fingers were never as good as a thick, hot cock, but in his mind, the fantasy was still playing where it was Ryan filling him up and taking him in hand, kissing his neck and shoulder, telling him he was gorgeous and tight and perfect. Luca's breath was ragged in the steamed-up room, the water still scorching and pounding down on his flesh.

He didn't eke out the climax, aware he didn't have long in total privacy. Instead, he chased it eagerly, letting the orgasm build and wash over him until suddenly he cried out, his pleasure peaking and blacking out his vision. He gasped as he shot thick ropes of white cum into the bathtub, blinking as it mixed immediately with the shower water, washing down the drain.

Taking several deep breaths, Luca slowly came down from his high. He hummed and rubbed his hole and softening cock, massaging out the last of the orgasm. He felt energised and rejuvenated and only a tiny bit guilty that he'd abused thoughts of Ryan like that.

The man was a bloody hero. It was only natural that Luca would take that caring nature and apply it to an intimate fantasy. And now, hopefully, Luca had purged any inappropriate feelings from his system. When Ryan returned, Luca could greet him casually and perhaps just enjoy an afternoon of guy time with pizza and video games.

Luca sighed and turned off the water, then reached for his towel. It had been so long since he'd vegged out at home like that. His box room didn't have the space, and they'd chosen to turn the living room in the house into another bedroom to split the rent as many ways as possible. The idea of just chilling with Ryan for the afternoon was heavenly.

Was it too much to daydream that they might even become friends? Maybe Luca could be brave and ask for his number or Facebook details?

Shaking his head, he stepped out of the bath and continued to dry himself rigorously. He was getting ahead of himself. He needed to see how the next couple of hours went. Then maybe assess if he thought Ryan might want to meet up again.

Because Luca was already certain that was what *he* wanted.

6

RYAN

By the time Ryan had taken Briar around the green and was heading back to the flat, he'd pretty much convinced himself that Luca would have fled and Ryan was never going to see him again. Why would he stay? Ryan was being a dick and putting pressure on someone who was vulnerable and had just been through something pretty shit. By even thinking of Luca in a sexual way, he was being a terrible person.

But Ryan couldn't help it. His heart skipped a beat as he thought about this sweet guy who might be waiting for him back at home, and he quickened his steps, much to Briar's confusion. Ryan wouldn't jump to any conclusions or push too hard, but there had been *something* between them just now, right? He hadn't imagined that?

There was only one way to find out.

Briar grumbled as Ryan ran up the stairs to his flat, his heart in his throat as he fished out his key and thrust it into the lock. He opened the front door and, with a thrill of delight, heard the low rumble of the TV and saw Luca's trainers were by the door.

He was still there.

Ryan arched his eyebrows down at Briar, who finally caught up with him and looked back up at him, panting. "See," Ryan whispered and winked at the dog. "I told you. Nothing to worry about."

Briar sneezed at him, as if to say, "You're an idiot, Dad", then bounded into the flat, eagerly looking for Luca.

Ryan knew the feeling.

It was stupid. When he'd written that note, he'd really meant it when he'd said it was okay if Luca wanted to slip away before Ryan's return. Indeed, that was what he'd been attempting to do when Ryan had come back from the gym. But now…Ryan was glad he hadn't disappeared without saying goodbye.

Or leaving his number.

Ryan shook his head at his own ridiculousness. But he couldn't remember the last time he'd felt his heart sing for someone like this.

"Hey!" he called out, hoping he sounded casual and not like he'd raced Briar around the green, anxious to get back in case Luca was going to vanish.

"Hey!" the now familiar voice called back from the living room.

Ryan kicked his shoes off and went to go find his guest lying on the couch, watching a documentary about the rainforests. The jogging bottoms Ryan had given Luca from his sister fit Luca perfectly, slung low on his hips, revealing a strip of skin where the T-shirt Ryan had also found for him had ridden up. God, that skin looked lickable.

Luca rubbed his eyes and looked from the telly to Ryan as he petted Briar's head. "Did you have a nice walk?"

Briar barked as if to tell Luca just what fun he'd missed out on. Ryan meant to say it had indeed been nice. The sun was shining, and it hadn't been too busy. Instead what spilled from his mouth was an excitable, slightly breathless, "You're still here?"

Luca tilted his head as they looked at each other. There was that pull again, that magnetism. Then Luca licked his lips. "Well, yeah," he said mischievously. "I'm not going to leave before pizza, am I?"

Ryan barked out a laugh, which made Briar bark for real and Luca grin. God damnit. He was cute *and* funny. It was an understatement to say Ryan was glad he'd stuck around.

He flopped onto the other sofa and sighed. "It's not here yet? Man, I'm starving."

"Me, too," Luca said with a chuckle and nodded at the TV. "I had to distract myself. I hope you don't mind?"

"You using up precious electricity on adorable tree frogs?" Ryan asked, jerking his head towards the documentary currently streaming. "Yes, I mind terribly."

Luca snorted, his eyes crinkling. "All right, clever clogs." There was a knock at the door, making Briar bark. But Luca lit up like a Christmas tree. "Pizza!" he cried, throwing his hands in the air and jumping to his feet. Ryan watched him jogging down the hall and greeting the delivery guy cheerfully.

Ryan had liked Luca when he was shy and anxious. But now he was coming out of his shell, Ryan was starting to feel something more.

He was pretty sure he was really starting to *like*-like Luca. Whether or not that was going to be okay, he had no idea. But for that moment, when Luca was still at the door, Ryan rubbed his chest above his heart and allowed himself a small smile. This was kind of exciting.

Who knew where the day was going to take them?

7

LUCA

Bursting at the seams with pepperoni pizza, jalapeño poppers, chicken wings, and spicy potato wedges, Luca groaned and stretched out on the sofa, the games controller bouncing off his rounded belly. His character had just been killed – *again* – but he didn't mind. In fact, he kind of loved it. He'd forgotten how fun it was to lose yourself in a game with a friend.

Was Ryan his friend now? Luca hoped so. They'd had a brilliant afternoon so far, just lounging about, forgetting their worries as they made their avatars run around, casting spells and battling monsters.

However, every now and again, Luca would glance over to the kitchen and see his clothes hanging from the rack. They had to be dry by now.

But he didn't want to leave.

It didn't feel like Ryan was angling to kick him out anytime soon, though. He certainly hadn't made any comments to that effect. In fact, he kept making Luca tea and fussing that he was warm enough. At the first hint that Luca was actually a little chilly, Ryan came back with the most enormous hoodie for him to put on.

It smelled like Ryan. Luca wrapped himself up in it, feeling warmed through all the way to his heart.

Ryan also stretched and moaned, rolling his neck and making it click. "Urgh, I suppose I should take this mutt for a proper walk," he said with a sigh, raising his eyebrows at Briar. "What do you say, Mr Poopy Bum?" Briar immediately jumped up from where he'd been lounging on the floor, doing his best to steal bits of pizza crust when Luca and Ryan were too engrossed with their game.

A walk? Luca's stomach dropped. Well, that would be his cue to leave, wouldn't it?

Except Ryan turned to Luca and grinned. "Wanna come?"

Luca's heart flipped with hope and excitement. Ryan didn't want to say goodbye yet? "Sure," Luca managed to say without spluttering too much. "Give me a sec to change back into my jeans, though?"

"Totally," said Ryan warmly. "You might want to keep the hoodie on. It's sunny but it's a little nippy."

Luca didn't trust himself to talk, so he smiled as he rose to his feet and collected his clothes to get changed in the spare room. But once he closed the door, he clutched his hands to his chest, squeezed his eyes, and danced on his toes. Not only had Ryan invited him to stick around longer, but then he'd also insisted on Luca staying in this damn boyfriend hoodie?

Luca couldn't help it, his heart fluttered. Like, an actual physical sensation in his chest. How could he have had such a horrible start to the day, then be feeling like this by the afternoon? His already tender head reeled as he hastily changed out of Ryan's sister's stuff into his own jeans and T-shirt, still going commando as the thought of turning his underwear inside out was kind of icky.

Speaking of sisters, his own family were getting a little rowdy. He was pretty sure Florence, Fiona, and Maryanne still hadn't slept, and they were hounding him via WhatsApp. He'd promised them he was okay and being looked after, but no, he wasn't home yet. Once he'd pulled Ryan's hoodie back over his head, he opened up his messages again, taking advantage of a moment of privacy.

He was going to have to tell the truth if he was going to get them off his back.

The guy who rescued me last night was the bouncer. He's really nice. I'm still at his place...so stop cock blocking!

He added several crying-with-laughter emojis and hit send, watching the screen for a response. Sure enough, they all started typing immediately.

Oh, REALLY?!

You should have said, you bad boy.

Pics or it didn't happen.

Luca scoffed and pocketed his phone. He'd deal with them later. Right now, he didn't want to keep Ryan and Briar waiting.

Sure enough, they were both standing by the front door. And was it Luca's imagination, or did Ryan's face light up at the sight of Luca? "Ready?" Ryan asked eagerly as Briar tugged on his lead and whined.

Luca chuckled. "I might need my trainers on first," he said playfully, pointing at them. Ryan laughed and stepped back, giving Luca some room.

"Well, if you're going to be fussy about it," Ryan said with a wink.

Luca *loved* how easy the banter was between them. Mal had been so pedantic once the honeymoon phase had worn off, nit-picking everything Luca tried to joke about. Honestly, what had Luca ever seen in him?

Stepping out into the bright and breezy afternoon air, Luca inhaled deeply. He was feeling much better, presumably as whatever shit Malcom had slipped him was leaving his system. But it was obvious that some fresh air wasn't doing him any harm either.

"I never found out where you live," Ryan said as they ambled along the pavement. "Not that you should have told me or anything," he mumbled afterwards, rubbing the back of his neck. It was really cute how awkward he could be. It seemed Luca's first impression had been right. Ryan was kind of a dork, and it was adorable.

"No, that's fine," Luca said. Briar tugged Ryan's arm on his lead, keeping them at a fair pace as they headed towards wherever his usual walk was. "It's nothing special," Luca continued. "Just a house share in Hackney. I have the smallest room," he added with a shrug.

Ryan arched an eyebrow at him. "It's still a roof over your head that you pay for," he said. "That's impressive in this economy and this city."

Luca had never really felt about it like that before. "I guess so," he agreed. Then he scoffed. "I can't afford much more on my salary, so it'll have to do."

"What do you do?" Ryan asked. "Sorry, I don't mean to interrogate you." He laughed. Luca loved that sound. He was more than happy to answer Ryan's questions if it kept him smiling so beautifully.

But Luca never knew what to expect when he told people what he did. He'd met a fair few masc-for-masc gym bunnies who ran a mile at the hint of anything fem. Well, there was only one way to discover if Ryan was like that.

"I'm a tailor on Saville Row," Luca explained. "Still training, working under the shop owner. He's a genius. But the positions are so insanely hard to get. It's an honour to be where I am. Hopefully, one day I can have the opportunity to design for myself, but for now, I'm on the right path."

He was aware he was perhaps over-justifying what he did, but he was kind of desperate for Ryan to understand and not laugh at him. However, in that moment, Ryan was just sort of gawking at him.

"A tailor?" he repeated. "As in...you make suits. From scratch?"

"With a machine," Luca explained hastily. "Not by hand."

Ryan shook his head. "Yeah, I assumed with a machine. That doesn't make it any less impressive. I'm in awe. That's *so* cool!"

For some stupid reason, Ryan's words brought a lump to Luca's throat. To be fair, he was still feeling kind of rough from the previous night, but hearing Ryan gush with praise was a little much for Luca's fragile sensibilities just then.

"Yeah?" He didn't want to come across as insecure, but he needed to double-check he'd heard Ryan correctly.

As they turned off the pavement into a playpark, Ryan shook his head. "That's a real skill, mate. I get all my suits altered because they never fit off the rack." *I bet they don't,* Luca thought to himself. His eyes flicked up and down Ryan's incredible physique in what he hoped was a subtle glance. "But a good suit just makes you feel like a boss, right? Wow."

Confidence rushed through Luca. He couldn't have agreed more. He beamed and nudged Ryan's shoulder as they walked along the pathway, past the see-saw and climbing frame. "Are you angling for a private fitting," he said. There was no masking it that time. He was definitely flirting. And to his delight, Ryan winked back at him.

"Maybe," he said.

Their gazes lingered together, but then Briar barked loudly and yanked Ryan's arm so hard he almost pulled him off his feet. The moment broken, Ryan laughed and let Briar off his lead so he could run free. There were lots of kids in the park with their parents, but Briar was good and didn't disturb them.

"He's well trained," Luca commented.

Ryan beamed. "I've had him since he was a pup. He, well…" Ryan trailed off, making Luca wonder if he'd said something wrong. Ryan shook his head and sighed ruefully. "Sorry, there's no need to get depressed about it, not after all this time. I was with a guy – he was older, and I thought it was true love. We even got engaged. But then one day, it was like he got bored and went back to his ex." Ryan shuddered. "That guy was a real dragon, seriously high maintenance with such a temper. I have no idea…anyway. I don't care why my ex went back to him. As soon as I moved out, I got Briar so I wouldn't be lonely."

Luca was aware he was gawping as they pottered along the path into a more woodland area, the leafy trees swaying in the cool breeze. He was very much stuck on the idea that anyone would get bored with Ryan. Had that guy been insane?

"Briar is definitely better than any rubbish fiancé," Luca said hotly. "What a dickhead to propose and then just leave."

Ryan's smile seemed fond as he looked at Luca. "I think I dodged a bullet, to be honest. No point in clinging on to something just because you want it to be something it's not. If I was still with him, I wouldn't have…well, I might miss out on my *real* true love, mightn't I?"

"Good point," Luca said, trying to sound sage. It was cute how Ryan talked about true love. Luca had always just hoped he might be lucky enough to bump into someone he fancied enough and wasn't too annoyed by to try making a life together. But the way Ryan spoke of it was more magical.

More romantic.

They spent the rest of the walk meandering through the woodlands, chatting about this and that. Luca talked about his cousins and Ryan his sister. Neither of them had been on holiday lately, but they both had a top five they wanted to visit, including a historical tour down the river Rhine in Germany. Luca hadn't thought anyone else had really heard of that particular destination, let alone had it on their bucket list. For the briefest of moments, Luca had a vision of them going *together*, but that was just crazy.

It was so easy being with Ryan, though. Luca didn't want the day to end. However, the spell had to break at some point, and there was only so long Luca could impose on Ryan's hospitality. As they headed back towards Ryan's flat, Luca chewed his lip, feeling like he should be responsible and go home.

At least he steeled himself, determined to ask for Ryan's number. That wasn't weird, right? They'd hung out all day and probably spent more quality time together than Luca had with some of his regular friends. It would almost be weirder if they *didn't* swap numbers.

Still, by the time they were back at Ryan's building, there was an awkward silence between them, and Luca was feeling tongue-tied. He didn't know what to say that didn't sound needy. He glanced over at Ryan as they paused by the outside gate, catching each other's eye.

Luca took a deep breath, then said, "I guess I should finally get out of your hair."

Just as Ryan said, "Would you like to stay for dinner?"

They blinked at each other. "Dinner?" Luca repeated, his heart in his throat. Did Ryan really want to keep spending time with him? Wasn't he bored already?

As Luca had only just thought – he *certainly* wasn't bored of Ryan. Who could be?

"Um." Ryan shifted on his feet. Briar was looking up at them both, swinging his big head from one to the other, probably confused as to why they weren't going inside. "No, sorry. You want to get home. I was just…never mind."

Luca bit his lip, not sure what he should say. He decided

to not overthink it and go with his gut. "I'd love to stay," he said earnestly. "I just feel like I've imposed on you all day. But if I'm welcome…" He trailed off, uncertain of where he was going with that sentence. But Ryan's face split into a dazzling smile.

"You're not imposing," he said emphatically. "I'm having a great day! Are you having a great day? It sort of feels like, uh…"

Luca laughed and touched the back of Ryan's hand, brushing it with his fingertips. "I *am* having a great day. Although I'm not sure I'm hungry just quite yet," he teased.

Ryan snorted. "No, me neither. More games, though? Or we could find something trashy to stream?"

Luca sighed and tilted his head. His fairy tale wasn't quite done with yet, after all. "Sounds wonderful," he said.

8

RYAN

RIGHT. SO. BY SOME MIRACLE, LUCA WAS STILL IN RYAN'S flat, laughing at his dumb jokes and beating him at the latest Battle Spell that Ryan could never talk any of his other mates into playing with him. They all preferred football or military games. But Luca was curled up on Ryan's sofa, in Ryan's oversized hoodie, cackling to himself every time he snuck up on a bad guy and blasted them with an exploding fireball.

Ryan was racking his brains for what to cook them later. He had a creamy chicken and asparagus thing that he usually cracked out for dates, but it had been so long since he'd had a guy around he was feeling rusty. Would Luca like that? Should Ryan cook it with rice or couscous? Or maybe he could try a spaghetti bolognaise?

"Mate!" Luca cried as Ryan's character died yet again through his lack of concentration. Ryan groaned and rubbed his eyes. His thoughts were all over the place.

"Maybe it's time for some trash TV?" he suggested.

Luca yawned and stretched his arms out. He was back in his own clothes now, and Ryan kind of missed the figure-hugging joggers and skinny tee he'd had on before. But

Ryan's hoodie that he'd lent him still rode up as Luca raised his hands over his head. God, Ryan wanted to touch that strip of skin so badly.

"Sounds brilliant," said Luca once he'd finished yawning. "There was a cheesy-looking magic academy show that I was thinking of trying, if that's your cup of tea?"

"Oh, I know the one," Ryan said enthusiastically. "It's got that guy in it from what's-it-called."

Luca snorted. "Yes, that's crystal clear now."

Ryan threw a cushion at him, making Luca squeal. Briar lifted his head and grumbled from his basket before going back to sleep. It was the simplest of playfighting, but Ryan's heart rate elevated immediately. Not to mention the fact that his cock twitched.

He cleared his throat. "Speaking of tea, do you want some? And maybe popcorn?"

Luca bit his lip, sending more delicious sparks down to Ryan's crotch. "Is it bad that after all that pizza I'd love some popcorn? I promise I'll eat whatever you make for dinner, too," he added hastily. "I feel like my stomach is going to turn itself inside out today."

He laughed, filling Ryan's heart with joy.

"Sure. Salty or sweet?" Ryan asked.

Luca licked his lips. "Sweet," he murmured.

Ryan's cock throbbed.

Oh *hell* fucking yeah, Luca was sweet.

A few minutes later, Ryan had made them tea from the kettle and hot popcorn in the microwave. Luca was apparently already knowledgeable enough with Ryan's entertainment system that he'd switched over from the games console to Netflix and got the TV show they'd been talking about up and ready to play. Ryan loved that he felt comfortable enough to do that.

So far that day, Luca had stuck to one couch, whilst Ryan

had given him some room and sprawled on the other. But now they were sharing popcorn, so Ryan tried not to overthink it as he dropped down beside Luca on the same sofa.

It was big enough that they weren't squashed together, but Ryan felt goose bumps flurry all over his body at the proximity regardless. Luca smiled at him as he helped himself to a handful of popcorn from the bowl between them. His feet were tucked under him as he leaned against the sofa arm, looking all cosy and comfy.

Like he belonged on Ryan's couch. In his flat.

In his heart?

Ryan cleared his throat and pressed play on the show, only half paying attention. It *was* pretty cheesy, and he was more interested in noting the way Luca was sitting next to him. Luca shifted a fair bit, eventually moving his legs to his other side so he could reach the popcorn easier.

Now, he was angled towards Ryan.

Ryan tried to focus on the newbie girl at the magic school and the obviously queer character, narrowing his eyes and silently threatening the show not to kill him off. Film and TV were getting better at not doing that, but it always made him a little nervous. He was so engrossed he wasn't looking as he reached for more popcorn, and his hand bumped into Luca's.

He got an immediate thrill from the contact, but he also gasped. "You're cold!" he exclaimed. Luca's hand was indeed icy, but Luca shrugged.

"I have crappy circulation," he said with a chuckle. "Never let me get lost on top of a mountain," he added with a wink. "I'll lose all my appendages, and some of them I *really* like." After getting over the shock that the Luca who'd seemed so nervous earlier had just made a crack about his dick, Ryan realised he must have seen some of the expedition photos he had on the wall. He liked the idea that

Luca was already getting to know Ryan enough to make in-jokes.

He also had another idea that he quite liked, but he'd have to see if it worked. He didn't want to put any pressure on Luca, but sometimes you just had to bite the bullet and take a leap of faith.

Ryan leaned over to the ottoman where he kept spare batteries for the remotes, and also a blanket for when he wanted to snuggle up on the sofa after a long day. Normally, it was just him and Briar, but today…

He moved the popcorn bowl and draped the blanket over his legs, holding it up and then raising his eyebrows at Luca. Without saying anything, Luca grinned and scooted over, spooning up to Ryan's side as they huddled under the blanket together.

Luca sighed and squirmed even closer, his eyes on the TV. But Ryan was unable to tear his gaze away from the cute guy now cuddled up next to him.

"Much better," Luca said contentedly. "I didn't realise how cold I actually was."

Ryan didn't trust himself to speak. He felt like he was in a dream and was too afraid of breaking the illusion if he wasn't careful. Instead, he rubbed Luca's arm and tucked the blanket up to Luca's chin where he was lying against Ryan's chest.

There was no chance Ryan was concentrating on the TV now. He was aware that the picture was moving and people were talking, but all his attention was now laser-focused on every breath Luca took, and how his now warmer body fitted perfectly alongside Ryan's. When he laughed at the show, Ryan could feel the rumble through his own chest.

Was this real? He'd only met Luca that morning, after all. Last night didn't count. But it felt like a hundred years had passed already and Ryan knew exactly who Luca was and how much he liked him. Was he reading too much into the tension between them just because their time together had been intense so far? Or had it been intense because the chemistry was pulling them that hard?

Luca looked up, catching Ryan staring down at him. Ryan expected him to laugh, that playfulness still driving the mood. But Luca's eyes widened ever so slightly, and Ryan's breath hitched.

Time seemed to slow down.

Luca's eyes were so green, like fresh spring grass, speckled with little flecks of brown. His breath ghosted over Ryan's mouth, making him shiver, and his body was warm and firm pressed up against Ryan's side.

Almost imperceptibly, Luca's fingers squeezed Ryan's hip.

Not sure who moved first, Ryan suddenly found his lips crashing against Luca's, the kiss desperate as their hands gripped each other tightly. Luca's hair was as soft and thick as Ryan had imagined it would be as he slid his fingers through it. Moaning, Luca clambered into Ryan's lap, the blanket falling away as they quickly discovered a new way to keep warm.

A small but persistent part of Ryan's mind wanted to check Luca was really okay with this after the fright he'd had last night with his ex. But Luca's hands were slipping under Ryan's T-shirt and rubbing his abs, so Ryan was pretty sure he was into it.

Into Ryan.

"Do you want to go to bed?" he rasped between kisses, nuzzling their noses together as Luca's fingers pressed into Ryan's sides.

"Oh, god, yes," Luca cried out, laughing as he kissed Ryan again. "Very yes, much now."

Ryan laughed as well, glad that playfulness wasn't all gone. Any doubts he had that he was pushing too fast vanished as he stood up with Luca in his arms, Luca's legs wrapped around his waist. He didn't worry about turning the TV off. He had more pressing matters at hand.

"Holy *fuck*, you're so hot," Luca moaned, kissing Ryan's neck and sucking on his collarbone. "Take me to bed, *please.*"

Ryan was so turned on, his cock throbbing in his jeans, that he was almost tempted to start getting naked right there on the couch. But even though Briar was sleeping, that felt weird with him there, so Ryan did as Luca had begged and carried him down the hall and into his room.

He would never have guessed this was how their day was going to turn out, but now they were here, falling onto Ryan's bed, he couldn't imagine it any other way.

9

LUCA

THIS WAS HAPPENING. IT WAS *REALLY* HAPPENING. LUCA HAD been fantasising about Ryan all day, and now he was on his bed. Hands were wandering. Lips were red and plump. Breaths were short and quick.

Fucking hell, he wanted *everything*.

Frantically, he grappled with Ryan's zip, doing his best to free his cock whilst Ryan was kissing his lips. He wanted to feel him in his mouth, in his arse, any way Ryan wanted to take him.

Luca had to laugh. When he'd pictured getting lucky last night, it had been maybe a quickie with a stranger in the loo at the pub. This was a million times better.

As Luca finally managed to undo Ryan's jeans, he slipped his hand through the opening of his briefs to find his hard, hot cock, just waiting to be touched. Luca squeezed the base, then rubbed the already leaking tip with his thumb, delighted with the guttural moan Ryan let out.

"Come on," Ryan said, nipping Luca's ear lobe. "I didn't spend all this time getting you warm to let you cool down now. Into bed with you."

Luca laughed and kissed the little love bite he'd been working on. "Do you have a condom?"

Ryan blinked, his face falling. "I don't know if they're in date…" he began.

But Luca shook his head and pecked him on the lips. "Not to worry! I brought one just in case for last night." He bit his lip and took a moment to be serious. "This is so much better than a bathroom hook-up."

Ryan caressed the side of his face, his expression tender. "*So* much better."

With another kiss, Luca slipped off the bed and scampered back to the spare room. He wasn't so embarrassed about having that condom on him now, he mused. In fact, he was pretty ecstatic over it.

He closed Ryan's bedroom door as he dashed back to him so Briar didn't interrupt them. The room was warm, with wooden furniture, earthy decorative tones, and lush green houseplants. Luca would hopefully get a chance to inspect it properly later, but in that moment, all he was interested in was re-joining the man who was holding the covers back for him.

Luca dove in, squirming against Ryan and kissing him passionately as Ryan dropped the duvet back down. They pressed the condom between their palms for a few moments as they held hands. "Do you want to bottom?" Ryan asked sincerely. Luca appreciated that he didn't just assume.

"I like both," he said truthfully. "But right now, yes, I'd love to bottom."

Ryan beamed. "Exactly how I feel," he said, a light relief to his words. "I'd love to top…this time."

Luca's heart flipped over. "This time," he repeated faintly before capturing Ryan's lips for a searing kiss. *This time.*

Yes. Luca decided already that he'd very much like there to be a *next* time.

Snuggled under the covers, kissing sloppily, they worked together to shove down their jeans and kick them off. But Ryan was right. Luca wanted to be hot, not just warm, and it felt so right keeping Ryan's enormous hoodie on as they rutted their hard cocks together, half dressed and safe under the duvet.

Luca's heart throbbed as much as his dick, feeling happy and free in Ryan's arms. There was nothing to prove, no one to impress. Just two men coming together in a joyous moment of intimacy.

Ryan manoeuvred them so they were side by side, Ryan spooning Luca from behind as he kissed his neck and stroked his weeping length, just the way Luca had imagined in the shower earlier. Considering he'd already come a few hours ago, it was remarkable how turned on he was again. He was trembling and gasping, muttering nonsense as he clutched onto Ryan's strong arms, pressing his back against Ryan's solid chest. Even through their clothes, Luca could feel all his bulging muscles.

He was in a dream. One he didn't want to wake up from. Luckily, he didn't have to.

Ryan had his cock between Luca's thighs, thrusting in time with his strokes on Luca's member. "Do you want me to fuck you like this?" Ryan murmured, sending a jolt of electricity straight to Luca's balls.

Luca took Ryan's hand that wasn't on his dick and lifted it to his mouth to suck his index and middle fingers. "I want you to fuck me *every* way, baby," he said, feeling devilish. "Why don't you finger me like this, then flip me onto all fours?"

Ryan growled and bit Luca's shoulder, the slight zing of pain making Luca gasp exquisitely. "Perfect," Ryan told him. Then he reached over to the bedside cabinet, opening one of the drawers to retrieve a tube of lubricant with a floral label on.

Luca giggled. "Rose scented, huh?" he teased. "I haven't seen that before."

Ryan grinned and kissed him on the mouth as he squeezed some onto his fingers. "Yep. It's like fucking a Turkish Delight, darling."

Luca snorted at such a ridiculous idea, but his laughter was cut off with a moan as Ryan's wet fingers slipped between his cheeks and caressed his entrance. Luca nodded, kissing along Ryan's jaw. "I can take two. Need you inside me, now."

Without preamble, Ryan did as Luca had asked, pushing two of his fingers inside Luca's hole as Luca shivered and concentrated on relaxing. He turned his head so they could kiss, panting a little as Ryan pushed his fingers all the way in and stroked Luca's prostate. This was vastly superior to Luca's own effort in the shower earlier. He couldn't believe he'd imagined taking Ryan's cock instead of his own unimpressive finger, and now he was going to get it.

He nodded, touching the side of Ryan's face, feeling his prickly stubble. "I'm good," he said breathlessly. "Stretch me with your cock. I can take it. Want you."

Ryan hummed as he kissed Luca and plucked the condom and lube back up. "Want you too, beautiful."

Luca buried his face into the side of Ryan's neck and grinned. He wasn't the most fem guy out there, but he liked being called beautiful under the right circumstances.

This definitely counted as the right circumstances.

With Ryan's sheathed cock and Luca's hole nice and slippery, Ryan kissed the side of Luca's neck, urging him on to his stomach. Ryan put his knees in between Luca's legs, encouraging him to spread, then lined up his juicy cock. Luca watched over his shoulder as Ryan kissed down his spine, holding Luca's cheeks apart as he breached him with his hard dick.

Luca moaned, clutching the bed sheets for anchorage. It burned, but he knew it wouldn't take long for him to relax and adjust. He wanted this *so* badly.

Ryan gnashed his teeth and grunted. "You feel so good, Luca. *Yes,*" he hissed. Luca loved the way his name sounded on Ryan's lips like that. They rubbed their scratchy cheeks together and kissed messily. Ryan took it slowly until he bottomed out, giving Luca the time he needed to accept him deep inside.

Luca rolled his hips, encouraging Ryan on. "More," he begged, wanting to feel every inch of him not just now but tomorrow as well. "Hard. *Please.*"

Luca shivered as Ryan withdrew almost all the way, then slid back in forcefully, just like Luca had asked for. He slammed into his prostate, making Luca wail and writhe. They undulated together, joining again and again as their pace sped up. Luca ground his throbbing cock against the mattress, pushing against Ryan's every stroke, chasing his orgasm. He'd meant it when he'd asked Ryan to fuck him six ways from Sunday, but he could tell both their needs were too great. It would be mad to switch positions now, so Luca just went with it, loving how Ryan was grabbing his hips as he sped up. Luca had left him a love bite, after all. Hopefully, Ryan would return the favour with a few cute finger bruises.

The only sounds that filled the room were their slapping skin and ragged breaths. They were both sweaty, and the scent of their musk lingered in the air as Luca gasped. Ryan pulled his hips up slightly, positioning his arse just right so every touch to his prostate was like fireworks. Luca cried out, feeling Ryan's franticness.

"Luca!" he yelled. Then he arched his back, slamming his

cock as deep as he could inside Luca, filling the condom with his cum. His grip on Luca's hips and thighs might have been brutal, but as he caught his breath, he kissed sweetly down Luca's back, gently stroking Luca's ribs and the tops of his legs. When his knuckles grazed Luca's hard, still leaking cock, he groaned.

"It's okay," Luca said, panting as he quickly gathered his wits. "I can finish it off."

But Ryan hummed and kissed the base of Luca's spine, carefully extracting himself. Luca blinked, his vision a little hazy as Ryan removed the condom, tied it off, then threw it over the side of the bed. "No, baby," Ryan murmured, easing Luca onto his back. "I'm taking care of you."

Luca bit his lip and caressed the side of Ryan's face as he nuzzled Luca's cock with his nose and cheek. He was most *definitely* taking care of Luca. Ryan slipped his lips over the length, swallowing Luca down to the root and sucking deliciously. Luca cried out, tugging at Ryan's soft dreads, urging him on. It wasn't going to take long.

But Ryan was a tease, speeding up, then slowing down, eking out Luca's climax as much as he could. Luca wriggled and thrust, fucking Ryan's mouth, desperate for release. Eventually, Ryan gave it to him, pinning his hips down and deep throating him with gusto. "Ryan!" Luca warned, but Ryan didn't stop. If anything, he sucked harder, and within seconds, Luca was shooting his load for the second time that day.

It was much better when someone else was making him come.

Boneless, he flopped against the mattress, breathing heavily and blinking his eyes until he stopped seeing stars. Ryan crawled up his side, flinging the duvet over them both again where it had slipped down. Luca barely had the energy to turn and smile as Ryan wrapped him up in his arms, squeezing him gently as they kissed. Luca tasted his own intimate flavour on Ryan's lips and loved it.

"My knight in shining armour," he mumbled happily.

"Damn right," said Ryan with a happy sigh. They closed their eyes and snuggled blissfully together.

"I've had the best day," Luca said sleepily. "Which is mental, considering how it started."

Ryan chuckled, nodding against Luca's neck. "The best," he agreed. "So glad you stayed."

So was Luca.

In fact, he was hoping he could stay for a long time.

Maybe even forever.

EPILOGUE

LUCA – EIGHTEEN MONTHS LATER

LUCA BREATHED IN DEEPLY AS THE SNOW FELL FROM THE afternoon sky, looking around the magical scene before him. The winding cobbled streets were glowing with fairy lights, and the scent of pine needles and cinnamon hung in the air. Quaint wooden signs hung over shops that were hundreds of years old, all selling handmade wares and shiny Christmas decorations. He couldn't read any of the German all around him, but that didn't stop him from marvelling at the beauty of the stained-glass windows and wrought-iron weathervanes on top of angular slate roofs.

He turned excitedly, beaming at Ryan, not quite believing they were finally here, taking their river cruise along the Rhine, exploring the Christmas markets as well as the enchanting forests and ancient castles.

This was the dream he and Ryan were still living, the one he'd never had to wake up from.

Ryan was grinning at him. "What?" Luca asked sheepishly with a giggle. He was perfectly aware that he was giddy and not just from the sweet brandy coffee that Rüdesheim was famous for.

Ryan brushed back Luca's hair from his forehead and smiled so fondly it made Luca's heart ache with happiness. "I just love seeing you so excited," he murmured, slipping his arm around Luca's waist. Even through his thick coat, Luca could feel Ryan's strength. He was always there to hold him, to protect him.

His knight in shining armour.

"I love going on adventures with you," Luca said in reply, leaning in for a chaste kiss. "Thank you."

It had been the easiest thing in the world to entwine his life with Ryan's. Since that first, surprisingly perfect day together, it had hardly taken three months before Luca had moved into Ryan's place with him. Ryan insisted he only pay a fraction of the rent and bills whilst Luca was still doing his apprenticeship, and had turned the spare bedroom into more of a workroom for Luca's fashion creations.

But Luca had insisted on paying his own way for this holiday, the one they'd been dreaming of for months and months from their shared bucket list. It felt good to know he'd earned his own ticket, and now he was in a magical wonderland with his gorgeous boyfriend, feeling like anything was possible.

Mostly Christmas shopping for all their friends and family. Good lord, he was glad he'd brought an empty suitcase with him. But for now, he and Ryan were enjoying some time just for the two of them. Luca's cousins were getting sick with jealously from all the happy couple photos he kept posting, but secretly, he knew they were thrilled he'd met someone so special.

Ryan squeezed his side. "Come on," he murmured, his lips cold against Luca's ear. "I want to show you something."

Curious, Luca followed Ryan down what could be considered the main street of the town, but it was as narrow and crooked and filled with wonder as Diagon Alley. Every little adjacent street was even narrower and packed with more quirky shops and bars. Luca and Ryan held hands, only pausing to buy a couple of gingerbread men to nibble on. It was a good job Ryan was also Luca's informal personal trainer with the amount he loved to feed him. Luca hadn't even had to ask for a cookie. Ryan had just seen him glance over at the sweet treats before buying them one each.

Luca grinned, the ginger warm on his tongue as he absorbed every little detail he could. There was only so much time he wanted to spend spamming his Instagram. The rest of this holiday, he wanted to be fully present with Ryan. Especially in their small cabin on the riverboat, where the walls were so thin, they'd had to practice being *super* quiet. But that was part of the fun, how wild they could drive each other, almost daring the other to slip up and yell or squeak. Luca was getting hard, just thinking of the tricks he was planning on deploying later.

When it came to Ryan's pleasure, there weren't any lengths he wasn't willing to go to. And Ryan felt the same, Luca knew. Even after all this time, they were still finding new ways to touch and delight each other. Luca hadn't known he could be this happy.

They came upon a little square on their left that Ryan led them into. There was some sort of ticket office that Luca realised was for the cable car. "Oooh," he said excitedly as they approached. There was still enough daylight that they'd be able to appreciate the view from the top of the impressive hill that Rüdesheim stood beside.

After he'd picked up their tickets, Ryan pointed upwards. "See her, up the top?" he asked, indicating the huge statue of a woman surrounded by angels, looking like she was ready for battle. "She was built to commemorate the unification of Germany. She's bad ass."

Luca grinned at Ryan, loving how quickly he could slip

into nerd mode. "If I didn't know you better, I might almost get jealous of your thing for bad-ass women with swords."

Ryan hummed. "Hmm, Eowyn," he said dreamily, reminiscing about his favourite Lord of the Rings character. Luca lightly smacked his arm, and they both laughed as they made their way to the cable car.

The view was even more breath-taking as they ascended over the vineyards on the side of the hill. Looking up showed Luca the mist-drenched forest surrounding the monument. Looking down, he took in the vista of the sparkling Christmas market town and the expansive Rhine river, winding its way left and right.

"This is like a fairy tale," Luca whispered, threading his fingers with Ryan's gloved hand.

Ryan hugged his side and followed his gaze out over the town. "Every day's a fairy tale with you, my prince," he said playfully.

Luca chuckled and shook his head. "So cheesy," he lamented.

He wouldn't have Ryan any other way.

At the top of the hill (which felt more like a mountain to Ryan, it was so high) there was a big bandstand with columns twenty feet high. Luca ran up to it, leaning against the cold stone as he sighed and looked out over what felt like the whole of Germany.

"Stay there," Ryan said in his ear. "I'll take an Insta boyfriend photo of you from behind."

Luca snorted, unable to help himself being childish. "You know I love it when you take me from behind."

Ryan's laughter was a low rumble as he hugged Luca, then sighed deeply. "I love you *so* much," he said quietly. He sounded almost sad or worried, confusing Luca a lot. Was everything okay?

"I love you, too, baby," he said, turning and cupping the

side of Ryan's face. But maybe he'd imagined the strange tone because Ryan gave him a beautiful smile and gently kissed his lips.

"Go on. Turn around."

Luca did as he was told, feeling a little silly as he posed, leaning against the column, gazing out over the stunning vista. "Is this all right?"

For a second, Ryan didn't respond. Then he cleared his throat. "Okay. You can turn back around now."

Luca laughed, already imagining how his cousins were going to tease him for being pretentious. But he experienced a moment of confusion, as Ryan was no longer standing in front of him.

He was down on one knee, holding up a ring box.

Luca gasped, his hands flying to his mouth as tears sprung in his eyes. "Ryan?" he whispered.

Ryan grinned, his own eyes glassy. "Uh…" he said, visibly collecting himself. "As we both love the cheesiness, um…" He took a deep breath, then held out one of his hands. Luca dropped one of his into it, gripping it tightly. "This knight would like to ask his prince if he'd live happily ever after with him. Luca, will you marry me?"

Luca squealed louder than he ever had for a pizza delivery man, dropping to his knees and flinging his arms around Ryan's neck. "Yes! Yes! *Yes!*" he cried as his tears sprung free, rolling down his cold cheeks. "Oh my god, I can't believe this is happening! *Yes!*"

Ryan wrapped his arms around Luca's back, letting out a deep cry of happiness against Luca's neck. Then they were kissing and holding each other, still kneeling on the damp ground like a couple of idiots.

"You're the best – the *craziest* – thing to ever walk into my life, darling," Ryan said as he showed him the dazzling band of diamonds.

"I can't believe I woke up to my happy ending that day," said Luca, laughing and crying as he let Ryan slip the ring on. It was perfect. "And now I get to wake up next to you forever."

"Forever and ever," Ryan agreed.

As they hugged together on top of the windswept hillside, Luca couldn't believe that fate had brought them here. And yet at the same time, he didn't see how they could possibly be anywhere else. This was a dream that they'd brought to life, and Luca wouldn't have had it any other way.

THANK you for reading Luca and Ryan's story, I hope you enjoyed it! To keep up with all the latest news, enter giveaways, read WIP teasers, and have the opportunity to get ARCs of new releases, please join my Facebook group, Helen's Jewels.

For more Helen Juliet books, please visit www.helenjuliet.com

For more books and freebie shorts from my American pen name, HJ Welch, please go to www.hjwelch.com.

Thank you to my team!

Cover Design: Cate Ashwood

Beta Reading: Amy Pittel

Proof Reading: Tanja Ongkiehong

General Awesomeness: Cheesebags (Ed, Amelia, and Conrad)

ALSO AVAILABLE

Thorn in His Side

The last thing beautiful, inexperienced Joshua Bellamy wants is an arranged marriage with the terrifying Darius Legrand. But if Joshua wants to save himself and his family from being thrown onto the streets by Darius's father, he has no choice. However, when Darius goes to extreme lengths to rescue Joshua from near-death, Joshua has to wonder if there's more to his beastly husband than he previously thought.

Former Captain Darius Legrand is used to being manipulated by his cruel father, but when Joshua is dragged into the feud between their families, he decides something has to change. Protecting Joshua is one thing, but Darius knows that falling in love can't be an option. Someone so young and beautiful could never give his heart to an older ill-tempered brute like Darius.

Joshua is determined to bring joy to Darius's life again, and Darius refuses to let Joshua hide his sweetness from the world any longer. Over time, it becomes clear that despite their differences, their hearts are drawing closer together. But can happiness ever be possible for a rose and a thorn when Darius's father will go to any lengths to see his deadly game through?

Thorn in His Side is a steamy, standalone MM romance novel featuring tender bubble baths, a stubborn but loyal horse, thunder storms, enough healing touches to mend any broken heart, and a guaranteed HEA with absolutely no cliffhanger.

Click here to get the Thorn in His Side eBook

Coming Soon: Thorn in His Side audio

ALSO AVAILABLE

Without a Compass

Riley Anderson has always been smitten with his older brother's best friend, Kai Brandt. But Kai is straight and he and Riley have nothing in common. Riley's a desk jockey and hunky Kai is obsessed with the great outdoors, just like the rest of Riley's family. It's bad enough that Riley is forced to go camping for his dad's 50th birthday. Even worse when gorgeous Kai shows up too and Riley isn't sure how long his crush will remain secret.

Kai always liked his best friend's cute but shy little brother. When they reunite after a few years apart, Kai is surprised to find that Riley has grown up…and Kai can't get him out of his head. Maybe now that Riley is an adult they can be friends?

When their camping trip takes an unexpected turn, Kai and Riley find themselves stranded together out in the wild. The chemistry between them is undeniable. But Riley is too afraid to believe this could be real, even though Kai knows this is no longer just about friendship for him.

They don't have long before they will have to rejoin civilisation. Can they face the truth in front of them before their lives pull them apart once more?

Without a Compass is a steamy, standalone MM romance novel with campfire kisses, a dog with a mind of her own and a guaranteed HEA with absolutely no cliffhanger.

Click here to get the Without a Compass eBook

ALSO AVAILABLE

Glitter on the Garland

Matt Bartlett's Christmas could use a little sparkle this year. Lucky for him, his extravagant gay best friend Aedan Gallagher arrives on his doorstep on Christmas morning, bringing with him a much-needed blast of festive cheer. Unknown to Matt, Aedan has been holding a torch for his best friend for years.

Matt and his family have been pulled apart in the last year by his dad's affair and the subsequent divorce. Now Matt and his younger sister are expected to play nice and share the holidays with his dad's new family. Aedan vows to stay by Matt's side, though, no matter what.

As they navigate Matt's vindictive step-mother and Aedan's own family trouble, Matt starts to realise that Aedan might be more than just a friend to him. He just doesn't know whether he should – or even can – take the next step for the first time, because then he'd have to accept something about himself he's afraid to admit...

Glitter on the Garland is a steamy, standalone MM romance novel featuring lots of prosecco, even more glitter, a reunion with a beloved dog, kisses in the snow and the best Christmas present of all. With a guaranteed HEA and absolutely no cliffhanger.

Click here to get the Glitter on the Garland eBook

ALSO AVAILABLE

Sparkle to the Season

Aedan wants everything to be just perfect for his boyfriend of seven years, Matt, for their first Christmas in their new home. But it's Christmas Eve and he's running out of time to create an idyllic winter wonderland. To make matters worse, Matt's present hasn't arrived.

A misunderstanding means the holiday might be ruined before it even begins. But little does Aedan know, Matt has a surprise or two of his own up his Christmas sweater sleeve.

Sparkle to the Season is a short, free and steamy sequel to Glitter on the Garland, although it can be read as a standalone, so long as you enjoy happy ever afters.

Click here to get the Sparkle to the Season eBook

ABOUT THE AUTHOR

Helen Juliet is a contemporary MM romance author living in London with her husband and two balls of fluff that occasionally pretend to be cats. She began writing at an early age, later honing her craft online in the world of fanfiction on sites like Wattpad. Fifteen years and over a million words later, she sought out original MM novels to read. By the end of 2016 she had written her first book of her own, and in 2017 she achieved her lifelong dream of becoming a fulltime author.

Helen also writes contemporary American MM romance as HJ Welch.

You can contact Helen Juliet via social media:
Newsletter (with FREE original stories) – https://www.subscribepage.com/helenjuliet
Website – www.helenjuliet.com
Facebook Group – Helen's Jewels
Facebook Page – @helenjulietauthor
Instagram – @helenjwrites
Twitter – @helenjwrites